P9-DUX-493

Just Like Daddy

Just Like Daddy

© 2015 Ovi Nedelcu

All rights reserved. No part of this book may be reproduced in any manner in any media, or transmitted by any means whatsoever, electronic or mechanical (including photocopy, film or video recording, Internet posting, or any other information storage and retrieval system), without the prior written permission of the publisher.

Published in the United States and Canada by POW!
a division of powerHouse Packaging & Supply, Inc.

ISBN: 978-1-57687-756-2
Library of Congress Control Number: 2014948085

powerHouse Packaging & Supply, Inc.
37 Main Street, Brooklyn, NY 11201-1021
info@POWkidsbooks.com
www.POWkidsbooks.com
www.powerHouseBooks.com
www.powerHousePackaging.com

First edition, 2015

10 9 8 7 6 5 4 3 2 1

Printed in China

Just Like Daddy

DISCARD

OVI NEDELCU

POW!
Brooklyn, NY

3 A
2 B
1 C

Morning is my favorite time!

When I wake up I'm rested and excited to see the sunrise!

Just like Daddy.

I get dressed in my super outfit, ready to take on the day!

Just
like
Daddy.

But before I head out on my adventures, I make sure I eat a big, healthy breakfast.

Just
like
Daddy.

HEALTHY
CRISPS!
MADE WITH
ORGANIC
TREE BARK!

FORMULA

After
breakfast,
I get in my car,
thrilled
to venture out
onto the open road
on my way
to work.

Just
like
Daddy.

Gg Hh
Ii Jj Kk Ll Mm Nn Oo

Once I get to work, I have
so much fun
doing all of
my projects.

Just
like
Daddy.

MARSHALL
LOBEL
LIONNI

After dinner, I like to open my books and have a few good bedtime stories to take my mind off a hard day's work.

Just like Daddy.
TAXES
PHONE BILL
FEE
JURY DUTY
ENDLESS FEES
VOTE FOR ME

CREDIT CARD
BILL
HIDDEN
FEES
$DEBTS

And when we go to bed,
we dream about the weekend.
FORMULA

ENDLESS
FEES
VOTE FOR
ME

Together.

To my family.

-OM